Lessons from the Hundred-Acre Wood

Lessons from the Hundred-Acre Wood

STORIES, VERSE & WISDOM

HALLIE MARSHALL
ILLUSTRATED BY JOHN KURTZ

DISNEY
PRESS

Book design by Edward Miller.

Printed in the United States of America

Based on the Pooh stories by A. A. Milne (copyright The Pooh Properties Trust).

FIRST EDITION

1 3 5 7 9 10 8 6 4 2

Library of Congress Catalog Card Number: 99-61290

ISBN: 0-7868-3243-6

Wherever they go, whenever, whatever they do
(even if they grow up), a boy and his bear
will always share something very special.

Contents

INTRODUCTION

The Hundred-Acre Wood has long been a place of enchantment. Possibilities live there, all sorts of adventures, stories that thrive and grow. It's the place where Winnie the Pooh and his friends can play forever and learn together. The lessons are mostly simple; sometimes, they're also profound. Pooh and his friends learn how to get along, how to be polite, how to share, how to (or how *not* to) track a woozle, how to get more from a hum. They also learn how to stand up for what they believe in, how to be good friends, and why it's important always to believe in yourself. There's plenty of time for fun, too, in the Hundred-Acre Wood. No one knows more about the power of laughter than Winnie the Pooh.

For who doesn't love Pooh? Who doesn't know someone like Rabbit? Or Kanga? Or sweet, gloomy Eeyore? Or the irrepressibly enthusiastic Tigger? The characters within the Hundred-Acre Wood embody recognizable human qualities, and in their gentle, funny way, they give us the opportunity to laugh at each other and ourselves. That is why their lives, their familiar mistakes, their mishaps, and their adventures so appeal to children and adults. When something seems to go wrong in that beloved forest, everyone knows everything will turn out to be fine. A partly cloudy day, after all, is always partly sunny.

Beneath the shelter of the Hundred-Acre Wood there are lessons to be learned, as well as friendships to share, songs to sing, hums to hum. Come join in the fun.

Humming Is Better
with a Friend

When Pooh woke up, he found that a hum had made itself up overnight.

> *Hum dee dum dee,*
> *Dah dah dum dee;*
> *Humdeedumdahdum!*

 Humming is a fine way to start the day.

Pooh hummed happily through breakfast, helped himself to seconds, and went to the door still humming. Since it was a mostly sunny morning, Pooh thought he would go out and share his hum with a friend. He thought about visiting Christopher Robin, and then he thought of Piglet.

He thought about Rabbit and Kanga and Tigger and Roo.
Because Eeyore was the last of his friends to be thought of,
Pooh set off at once to see him.

⋆ *Last doesn't really mean least.* ⋆

When he arrived at the Gloomy Place where Eeyore lived, Pooh called out, "Good morning!"

"Are you sure?" Eeyore looked at the sky. "Would you call that blue, Pooh? Or gray? At least it's not raining," he added. "Yet."

A mostly sunny day, to some,
can look a lot like partly gray.

Pooh didn't have an answer for that, so he went ahead and hummed his hum. When it was over, he waited for Eeyore to say it was a nice one—small, perhaps, but fine.

Eeyore didn't. Eeyore said, "I don't understand. There's a *hum dee dum* and a *humdeedumdahdum*. Why are there so many?"

"That's the way it came," Pooh told him.

"Well," said Eeyore, not unkindly, "don't worry, Pooh. Maybe it will come better next time."

Not everyone understands
where a hum comes from.

Pooh thought perhaps he'd better share his hum with himself for a while, so he walked to his Thoughtful Spot and sat thoughtfully down.

"Hello, Pooh!" said Rabbit.

"Hello, Rabbit," said Pooh.

Rabbit had a question. "What are you doing just sitting there, when there's so much to be done?"

"I was humming," Pooh said.

"That's all very well for some," said Rabbit.

"Do you want to hear it?" Pooh asked politely.

"I really must be going." Rabbit glanced up. "I'm too busy to hang about, and it looks like rain."

"Rain?" said Pooh. "Oh, dear. I'd better go home."

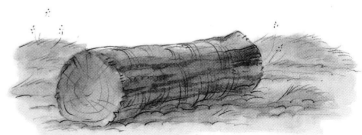

If no one wants to share your hum,
you can always share it with yourself.

Piglet knew a mostly sunny day when he was in one. He was outside Pooh Bear's door, trying to reach the bell, when Pooh himself came up.

"Here," said Pooh. "Let me do it for you." He knocked at the door and then remembered it was his own house. "Come on in," he said. "I think it's time for a little smackerel."

❋ Anytime is a good time for a smackerel. ❋

When he was round with honey, and Piglet had eaten some haycorns, Pooh thought to share his hum. The hum had taken shape by then, and Piglet helped a lot.

> *Oh . . .*
> *Humdee!*
> (Piglet sang.)
> *Humdeedumdahdum!*

A hum can grow much fancier when
a friend has time to help.

A Basically Blue Sky

Humdee

Dumdeedahdum

Humdeedumdahdum

Humdeedumdeedumdahdee!

It's a humdeedumdah morning,

A sweet humhummy sort of day,

All sunny except for a cloud or two

Coming over the treetops to play. . . .

The clouds are chasing, lazily

Racing, lacing through

A basically blue

And perfect

Sky.

Oh . . .

Humdee!

(Pooh sang.)

Humdeedumdahdum

Dumdeedahdeedumdum!

The clouds are chasing, lazily

Racing, lacing through

A basically blue

And perfect

Sky.

How to Track a Woozle

What kind of tracks
Would a woozle leave?
Or a wizzle—perhaps—
If a woozle it wasn't.

Following some mysterious tracks
can lead to an adventure.

On a white winter afternoon, Pooh and Piglet met some paw prints in the snow. "Do you think it's a woozle?" Piglet asked.

"It could be."

Pooh thought.

Pooh thought some more.

"Maybe or maybe not. It's hard to tell."

If you don't know something
for sure, you may as well admit it.

"Look, Pooh!" Piglet pointed ahead.

"Three woozles!" Pooh cried. "And one wizzle! Or a heffalump and a jagular. It's very hard to tell."

One more of whatever it was, was enough for Piglet. He was getting frightened, so Pooh made up something to cheer him.

A bracing hum may be soothing to
a small friend in scared circumstances.

Pooh's hum went like this, and Piglet put in the "whats."

We'll track these tracks
And turn this turn
Around this tree
Fearlessly! (Fearlessly?)
Then we will see . . . (What?)
What we will see. (What?)
And we will see . . . (What?)
What we will see. (What? What?)

A few well-placed "whats"
can be *just* the thing.

When they paused to consider another verse, the two friends heard someone calling. "What was that?" Piglet asked.

"Maybe it was a jagular," said Pooh. "Or maybe it was Christopher Robin."

And it was.

"Silly old bear," Christopher Robin said. "You went around and around that tree, with Piglet running after you. Whose paw prints were you following?"

When someone with brain poses a puzzle,
it's your job to think of an answer.

Pooh scratched his head. "Mine," he decided sadly. "Mine and Piglet's, too. I am a bear of no brain at all."

Christopher Robin hugged him tightly. "You're the most wonderfulest bear in the world."

It doesn't take brain to be wonderfulest.

On the way back toward Pooh's house, Piglet couldn't help asking, "You mean it was us all the time?"

"It was us." Pooh sighed. "I am a foolish bear."

"You're not foolish," Piglet said. "Maybe you're just hungry."

Pooh's face brightened. "I'm always hungry," he said.
"Well, almost always." He looked hopefully at Piglet. "Do
you suppose it's time for a little something?"

Piglet nodded.

A real friend (however small)
never lets you feel foolish for long.

Some time later, a somewhat sticky Pooh made up
another hum:

Was it a woozle?

Was it a wizzle?

Wizzle or woozle or——?

What was it really?

Really it was

A hungry old bear

And his daring

Friend Piglet.

"Was I daring?" Piglet asked.

"Very," Pooh Bear told him. "You stayed with me even though you were afraid to."

"Oh!" said Piglet. His face turned red. "Yes, I did, didn't I?"

Sometimes just being there takes courage.

Whose Tracks?

Whose tracks are those
In the snow-white snow?
Whose tracks are these
Here around the trees?

What kind of tracks
Would a woozle leave?
Or a wizzle—perhaps—
If a woozle it wasn't?

("I'd rather it wasn't,"
Our small Piglet said.
Pooh shook his head.
"Me, too," said Pooh.)

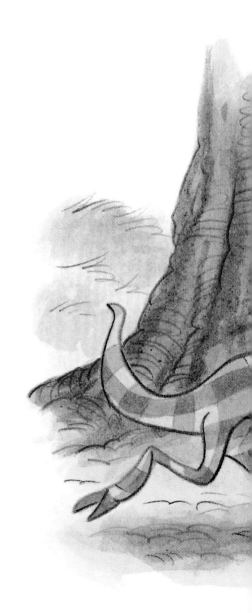

("There's one way to know."

Pooh looked at his friend.

"We'll follow these tracks

To find where they end. . . .")

We'll track these tracks, and we'll turn this turn,

Turn around this tree,

Fearlessly! (Fearlessly?)

Then we will see . . . (What?)

What we will see. (What?)

And we will see . . . (What?)

What we will see! (What!?)

What Tiggers Do Best

One morning, Kanga wanted to get things done around the house. So the first thing she did was send Tigger and Roo outdoors to play in the sunshine.

Tigger bounced along, going *BOING! BOING! BOING!* And Roo followed as well as he could: *boing boing boing boing!!!*

All that time, Tigger was talking about—tiggers. Tiggers could ice-skate and tiggers could swim, and they could climb trees even better than Pooh. Because a tigger could *bounce* from one branch to the next.

★ Tiggers think tiggers can do anything. ★

When they had gone to the top of a tree, Tigger remembered something. As good as they are at bouncing upward, tiggers don't like to climb down.

Tigger and Roo were stuck.

It's better to remember before going up
that you have a problem with down.

It was Christopher Robin who came up with a rescue plan. He took off his coat, and Kanga and Piglet and Pooh and Rabbit and he all held tight to the corners.

Roo jumped from a branch into the middle of the coat. "Whee!" he squealed. "Come on, Tigger, it's easy!"

Tigger looked down. "Jumping might be easy for jumping animals like kangas and roos, but it's different for bouncing animals like tiggers."

He held on to the tree for dear life.

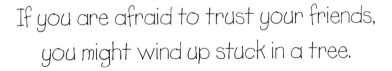

If you are afraid to trust your friends,
you might wind up stuck in a tree.

Then he slipped, and Tigger found out how easy going down was. Once he was safe on the ground, Tigger felt like bouncing with joy, and bouncing, and bouncing, and bouncing.

★ Sometimes the best thing to do is let go. ★

"But that's all wrong!" Rabbit threw his hands in the air. "One can't go bouncing everywhere! Someone might get hurt!"

Piglet nearly agreed. Tigger had a way of saying hello that almost always bowled him over.

"We have to do something!" Rabbit went on.

"But what?" Pooh asked.

"Shhhh," Rabbit shhhhed. "Don't talk. I need to think."

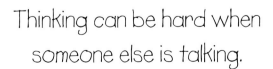

Thinking can be hard when
someone else is talking.

"I'll circulate a petition," Rabbit announced.

Pooh's eyes were partly closed. He was thinking of a hum, and was just deciding that "pounces" might sound nice with "bounces."

Words that sound nice together
make for a better hum.

Tigger sometimes

Pounces Rabbit

Or bounces me

Or Piglet or Roo

And occasionally Eeyore, too

(And . . . bother!

This isn't going anywhere!)

"Were you humming something helpful, Pooh?" Rabbit asked.

"No, no, not at all," Pooh said. "What were you saying, Rabbit?"

There are times when a
hum isn't helpful at all.

Pooh hadn't been listening, but Piglet had. "What kind of p-p-pet-petition?" he asked.

"Something to the effect that bouncing is bad," Rabbit answered. "Very bad. Very, very bad. Very."

Piglet said, "It's not *that* bad."

"Everyone will sign it, and the petition will be a Rule: NO BOUNCING!" Rabbit smiled at the thought. "Tigger will have to stop bouncing."

Piglet did a brave thing. He shook his head. "I won't."

Rabbit was surprised. "Won't what, little Piglet?"

"I won't sign a p-p-p-rule about bouncing. Tigger just *is* bouncy," Piglet explained. "He can't help it."

"Hmph," said Rabbit. But he didn't make a petition.

When very small piglets stand up to
rabbits, it counts as a very brave thing.

Sometimes "hmph" can mean "you're right."

I Bounce

Oh, if you could only know
How it feels to go and
Bounce and bounce and bounce;
To leave the earth
For a moment or so and
Bounce and bounce and bounce.

I bounce into sky—
Endlessly blue!
I bounce so high—
I FLY from this world
For a moment or two and I
Bounce and bounce and bounce!

Owl Talks About Brain

Back when I (Owl) was young,

Barely hatched, fairly new,

Way back then I was almost—

Almost as brainless as you

But I grew smarter as I grew

By the time I fledged I knew:

Some have brain and some don't.

Pooh had stopped by Owl's for a snack. He was feeling sleepy.

"Pooh!" said Owl. "Pay attention!"

"Yes, Owl," Pooh answered. "Yes, I am." That is what Pooh *said*, but this is what he was thinking:

Buzz, buzz, buzz, buzz, buzz, buzz

I wonder what that buzzing wuzz?

Buzzing often means bees,
and bees mean . . . honey!

The buzzing thing had buzzed a bit and then flown out the window. "I probably should be going," Pooh said. "Unless, of course, there's more."

Owl blinked. "I would think you'd had plenty."

Pooh thought perhaps he had. Though there was still one small rumbly place in his tumbly. He would have told Owl about it, but Owl was going on. Pooh waited to break in.

You should wait for a polite time to interrupt,
no matter what your tumbly tells you.

After a while Pooh's tumbly quieted down. He was having a hard time keeping his eyes open. Owl kept talking and talking and talking.

Rabbit has brain, as do (Owl) I,
And Christopher Robin . . . oh, my!
Tigger's brain is in his bounce.
(If you think bouncing counts)
Eeyore has brain, and Kanga, too,
And I have hopes for Baby Roo.
But you, dear Pooh, dear, dear Pooh,
Are a bear of so very little . . . Well!
Some have brain and some don't.

If one goes on long enough,
it gets a bit boring.

Pooh dozed off. He snored. And he dreamed. He dreamed he was a bee, buzzing from flower to flower, picking up pollen and flying it home.

Being a bee was hard work.

So Pooh dreamed he was Pooh again. He was opening a cupboard, taking down a jar. He dreamed he was eating, eating honey. Pooh smiled in his sleep.

After working hard, it's pleasant
to open the honey cupboard.

Then Pooh dreamed he was Eeyore (which wasn't much fun). He dreamed he was Owl, then Tigger, and for a moment he was Christopher Robin. Christopher Robin was saying, "Silly old bear."

And, in his dream, Pooh was suddenly himself again. He said, "Silly old Christopher Robin."

When someone calls you silly (in a nice sort of way), just call them silly right back.

Meanwhile, Owl was still talking.

I've forgotten Piglet.
He is so very small . . .
Can a piglet possibly
Have any brain at all?

If it doesn't take brain to be wonderfulest,
it shouldn't take size to be great.

Owl had been so busy chatting, he hadn't noticed Pooh's little nap. Pooh woke up and waited until Owl was done, and then he said good-bye.

On his way back through the Hundred-Acre Wood, Pooh stopped at his Thoughtful Spot. He thought: I'm lucky to be me.

Brain or no brain, life is
good when you're Pooh.

Some Have Brain

(A Duet of Sorts)

Back when I was young,
Barely hatched, fairly new,
Back then I was almost—
Almost as brainless as you
But I grew smarter as I grew
By the time I fledged I knew:
Some have brain and some don't.

Buzz, buzz, buzz,
Buzz, buzz, buzz!
I wonder what
That buzzing wuzz?

Some are born to think and ponder.
Others will simply wander about—
Here and there, wherever they please,
Singing things about birds and bees,
Some have heads all filled with fluff.
Some have Brain and some don't.

Buzzing meanz beez
(I mean, it means bees!)
Bees usually mean honey
And honey means . . . me!
Hurray for the life of a bear!

Pooh Learns More
About Bees

Pooh trotted all the way to Christopher Robin's house. "Honey!" he said, a little breathlessly, when Christopher Robin came to the door. "I'll need a balloon. And bring your umbrella."

Christopher Robin smiled at him. "Haven't we done this before?"

"Don't you remember?" Pooh asked. "Those were the wrong sort of bees."

If you don't succeed with the wrong sort of bees, it's worth another try with the right sort.

Christopher Robin held Pooh's paw as they walked
through the forest. Pooh held on to the balloon. When they
got to the base of a particular tree, Pooh said, "Let me go."

Christopher Robin let go, and Pooh floated
up, and up, and up.
Pooh pretended to
be a rain cloud.

Below him, Christopher Robin opened the umbrella. He glanced at the clear sky, at his round bear, and at the balloon. He felt a little silly as he said, "Tut, tut. It looks like rain."

Only an understanding friend will do
something for you he thinks is silly.

When a bee buzzed down to examine him, Pooh hummed a reassuring sort of hum:

"I know I look like a bear,
Though I'm a stray cloud,
Who accidentally blew here,
Who accidentally flew."

A reassuring hum to bees might be—
but, then again, it might not.

Another bee buzzed by, then another and another. "Christopher Robin?" Pooh called down. "These bees are suspicious. It's not working this time either."

Christopher Robin called back, "Perhaps you should try to distract them."

So Pooh waved a paw toward a distant treetop and went on singing:

"Somewhere over there,
There are more clouds,
All accidentally floating
Around. (Ow!)"

Bees don't care if you're there by accident . . .
they care about their honey.

One sting wasn't so bad. Such things sometimes happen to bears. Pooh was close enough that he could actually smell honey. He gathered his courage and started over:

"I know I look like a bear,
Though I'm a stray cloud,
Who innocently blew here,
I innocently flew. (Ow!)"

Apparently, bees have more
brain than one would think.

"Christopher Robin?" Pooh shouted. "*OW!* I think I'd better come down."

"Tut, tut," Christopher Robin said one last time. He folded his umbrella and held his arms out wide. "Jump!"

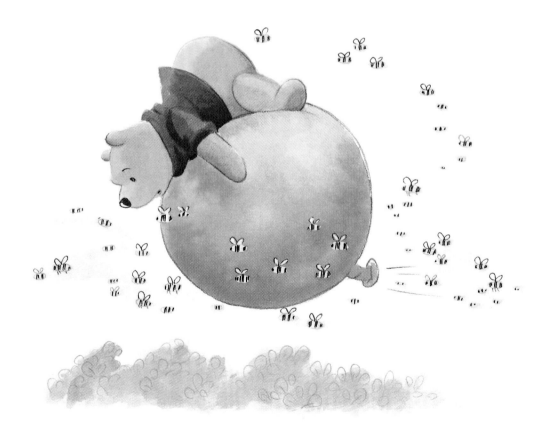

When you're surrounded by a swarm of
suspicious bees, it's best to take the leap.

Pooh let go of the balloon and went down. His fall wasn't graceful at all. As he turned over and over in the air, he thought: Bother. This is what comes of liking honey so much.

Liking something too much
can sometimes be a bother.

No one was hurt. Pooh Bear is stuffed full of fluff. When Christopher Robin caught him, it felt like catching a heavy pillow. "*OOOHfooh!*" they both said when Pooh landed. Christopher Robin sat down hard.

Pooh hugged him. "Thank you," he said.

Christopher Robin laughed. "Silly old bear."

"Silly old bear," when said the right
way, sounds just like "I love you."

Pooh's Reassuring Hum

I know I look like a bear,
Though I'm a stray cloud,
Who accidentally blew here,
Who accidentally flew.

I'm only one of a crowd
Of some innocent clouds,
Just innocently floating
Around. (Ow! OW!)

Somewhere over there,
There are more clouds.
All accidentally floating
Around. (Ow!)

I know I look like a bear,
Though I'm a stray cloud,
Who innocently blew here,
I innocently flew. (Ow!)

Learning About Manners

What goes up and up,
Usually comes down;
Up again, down again,
Up again, then down.

Roo giggled and reached for his toes. Pooh was teaching him an exercise song. "DOWN AGAIN!" Roo squealed.

"Roo, dear," Kanga said. "Can you keep it down?"

Roo tried. But it wasn't easy.

It's hard to keep it down and
to exercise at the same time.

"Roo!" Kanga pointed to a chair. "Maybe you should sit over here for a while." She looked at Pooh. "You, too."

Pooh sat at the kitchen table. He gazed hopefully in the direction of the cupboards. But Kanga didn't see him. She was doing something else.

If you stare at someone's cupboards,
she *may* offer you a little something.

"Tell the story of how you got stuck in Rabbit's doorway," Roo begged.

Kanga turned around very quickly. "Now, Roo, dear, don't be rude."

Pooh didn't mind. "Rabbit asked me if I wanted some lunch," he answered. "And I told him yes. It was a good lunch, a very good lunch."

"You ate so much and got so fat that you got stuck going out!" Roo yelled.

"Shhhh! Roo!" Kanga planted her paws on her hips.

When your mother puts her paws on her hips, you know you're in trouble.

"But he did!" Roo crowed. "He ate a whole lot."

"I did," Pooh agreed. "Rabbits don't always use doors. Sometimes they have tunnels into their houses. And I got stuck in Rabbit's back tunnel after I had lunch."

Kanga's paws still rested on her hips. But there came a knock at the door, a bouncy knock, and Kanga went to answer.

There is such a thing as being saved by the bell, or by a bouncy sort of knock.

"Hello, Tigger!" Roo cried. "Am I glad to see you!"

"And I'm glad to see you!" Tigger bounced over to Roo and gave him a hug.

"I'm trying to teach Roo some manners." Kanga sighed.

"I was learning an exercise song!" Roo yelled at the exact same moment.

Tigger looked from one to the other. "Manners are good," he said at last.

✶ Good manners are good. ✶

Pooh's tummy gave a tumbly leap when Kanga asked, "Would you like some lunch?"

"Yes, please," Pooh told her, "very much."

"Absolutely!" Tigger said. "Oh, yeah. Positively! Pause-eh-too-villy! Yes."

Roo was minding his manners. He said, "Lunch sounds nice, Mother Kanga." Then he grinned at Pooh. "You won't get stuck when you're through?"

"I hope not," Pooh said.

✳   There's always room for hope.   ✳

There was honey for Pooh, extract-of-malt for Tigger, and a well-balanced meal for Roo. Rabbit had sent some fresh carrots from his garden. There were sandwiches and cookies. Kanga was a great cook.

Pooh was in heaven.

★ Heaven is how you cook it. ★

Roo tried to sing while he was drinking his milk. He had to be patted on the back for a while, and then wiped off.

When he was dry and clean again, Roo went on with the song:

"Roundness is boundless;
So therefore, Pooh supposes,
He must stretch up and up,
Then reach for his toeses."

Tigger clapped. "Good show!" he said. Pooh laughed and Kanga smiled.

Manners are good, and so is singing
(as long as you're not drinking milk).

What Goes Up

What goes up and up,
Usually comes down;
Up again, down again,
Up again, then down.

(This holds true unless
You're spinning around;
Round and around again,
Up up again, and down.)

Roundness is boundless;
So therefore, I suppose,
I must stretch up and up,
Then reach for my toes.

What goes up and up
Usually comes down;
Up again, down again,
Up again, then down.

Rabbit's Big Plan

Rabbit's Rules

1. *No bouncing.*

2. *Don't eat so much at lunchtime*
   that you get stuck in my doorway.

3. *Don't talk while I'm thinking.*

4. *Keep out of my garden.*

5. *No bouncing in my garden.*

6. *Absolutely no bouncing allowed.*

7. *This means you!!!*

Thank you for your cooperation.

As a rule, rabbits don't much like bouncing.

"That should do it." Rabbit looked at his new sign. "Just seven simple rules anyone can follow."

The bounce came from behind him, and it knocked Rabbit flat. "Hello, Long Ears! It's me, Tigger! That's T-I—double Guh—Er!"

"I know how to spell." Rabbit sat up and pointed to the sign. "Can't you read?"

"Ah, yes," said Tigger, who maybe couldn't. "Very nice," he added. "So . . . uh . . . say . . . what are we going to do today?"

When in doubt, change the subject.

That gave Rabbit an idea. "Come back tomorrow," he said. "Tomorrow we're going to have an expedition."

"A what?"

"An expedition," Rabbit repeated. "An explore. Just for fun, of course."

"Oh, boy!" Tigger said. "Tiggers love to explore. Count me in."

 Whether they understand what or
why, you can usually count in a tigger.

Rabbit invited Pooh and Piglet over for a meeting. "I have a plan," he told them. "We have to take Tigger out and lose him."

"Lose him?" Pooh asked.

"Oh, we'll find him again," Rabbit said. "And he'll be so happy to be found that he'll be a smaller Tigger. A sadder Tigger. An Oh-am-I-glad-to-see-you Tigger. It will take those extra bounces right out of him."

A bouncing animal, when feeling sad or small, maybe won't bounce at all.

The next morning was chilly and misty. Rabbit lost
Tigger as planned. Then he lost himself and Piglet and Pooh.
He said, "Everything looks the same in the mist."

Piglet said, "We've seen that sandpit before."

"I was thinking . . ." That was Pooh. "As soon as we're
out of sight of this sandpit, let's try to find it again."

If you're looking for home but you keep
finding a sandpit, try looking for the
sandpit—and you might find home.

"If I was trying to find this sandpit, I'd find it," Rabbit claimed. "Rabbits don't get lost, and I'll prove it. I'll be right back."

He walked out into the mist, and he didn't return.

They waited for a long while, and finally Pooh said to Piglet: "Let's go home."

Piglet asked, "Do you know the way?"

"No," said Pooh. "But there are twelve pots of honey in my cupboards, and they are calling to me. I think we should listen to my honey."

If you listen to your honey (or your heart or tummy), it may call you back home.

Pooh followed his rumbly tumbly, and Piglet followed Pooh. They were safe.

But Rabbit was out in the Hundred-Acre Wood. The mist swirled around him. There were noises that scared him silly. Rabbit was talking to himself:

"Maybe losing Tigger wasn't a good plan."

"Maybe I've lost me."

"But rabbits don't get lost."

"Rabbits never get lost."

"Maybe this was a bad plan."

★ The best-laid plans aren't always. ★

Rabbit couldn't see Christopher Robin in such a situation. Or Owl. But he knew what Pooh would do. Pooh would make up a hum. So Rabbit tried that.

It's a cold and misty day
And I may have missed my way
Somehow
In this wet and misty day
I guess I missed the way
Somehow . . .

A bounce rolled him over and over, and Rabbit came up smiling. "Oh, TIGGER!" he cried. "I am glad to see you!"

The friend who finds you when you
might be lost is a very welcome friend.

It was a smaller rabbit that greeted Tigger, a slightly sadder rabbit. An Oh-I-am-so-very-happy-to-see-you sort of Rabbit.

"Hello, Long Ears," Tigger said. "Were you lost?"

"Rabbits never get lost," Rabbit told him. "I was here all the time."

You are where you are wherever
you are (that's got to be a rule).

As a Rule

It's a cold and misty day,
And I may have missed my way,
Somehow.
In this wet and misty day,
I guess I missed the way,
Somehow.

But I must have meant to be here,
Because rabbits don't ever get lost.
I know these woods.
I know that tree.
I've seen it before.
I've seen it before.

I know where I am.

But where am I?

As a rule . . .

Rabbits don't get lost.

Rabbits won't get lost,

As a rule . . .

Rabbits don't ever get lost.

Rabbits never never get lost.

So I must have meant to be here.

I meant to be here all the time.

I know these woods.

I know that tree.

I've seen it before.

I've seen it before.

I know where I am.

So where am I?

Where's Eeyore's Tail?

You think you can depend on tails.

You don't expect tails to go wrong.

The last I looked, it was right there.

Now when I look there . . . it's gone.

"Don't tell me," Christopher Robin said, "just turn around."

Eeyore turned and Christopher Robin asked, "Where did you lose it this time?"

Eeyore shook his head sadly. "I have no idea."

If your tail's not following you,
it follows that it's missing.

Christopher Robin told Owl and Rabbit about Eeyore's missing tail. While Owl talked (and talked) about where a tail might be (and where it might not), Rabbit went around to his friends and organized a search party.

Getting organized is sometimes
better than just talking about it.

Everyone joined in the search. From the tallest to the smallest, they combed the Hundred-Acre Wood.

The tail was not to be found.

And then Christopher Robin and Gopher accidentally fell into a deep pit.

Accidents happen.

Pooh and Piglet had dug that pit to try to catch a
heffalump. It had been so long before that everyone had
forgotten it. The trap was covered with broken branches and
leaves.

As Christopher Robin and Gopher crashed through, Christopher Robin hoped: *I hope I don't fall on him.*

If you're falling with a smallish friend, you have to hope you'll land first.

They landed with a thump, but safely. Christopher Robin began calling, "Help! Help!"

Gopher stamped his foot a few times. "Ground's too hard for digging," he said.

Soon Kanga and Roo and Tigger and Rabbit were there, then Piglet and Pooh and Eeyore and Owl. They gathered around the edge of the pit and looked down.

Christopher Robin looked up. "I think I could climb out of here," he explained. "But I don't believe Gopher can."

It's bad form to save yourself when somebody else needs your help.

Roo had an idea. "I saw a piece of rope back there, all twisted in the thistles," he squeaked. "We could use it to help rescue Gopher."

"Roo!" cried Christopher Robin when Roo showed him the rope. "You've found Eeyore's tail!"

It *was* Eeyore's tail, and it ended up being very useful. They used it to pull Gopher out of the pit.

 A tail can be more than an
extra bit at the back.

Christopher Robin got out of the pit by himself, then he fastened the tail back on.

Eeyore was incredibly happy. He wagged his very useful tail. He swished it from side to side. Eeyore actually frisked.

Roo was a hero. They all yelled, "Hip, hip, *Roo*ray! Hip, hip, *Roo*ray!" Eeyore and Gopher were especially loud.

You're never too young to be a hero. It may just take sharp eyes and quick thinking.

It Was There . . . Now It's Gone

You think you can
Depend on tails.
You don't expect tails
To go wrong.
The last time I looked
It was right there.
Now when I look there,
It's gone.

It was always
Just behind me,
Always tagging along.
A little something
at the back . . .

I thought it was there,
And it's gone.

At the back . . .
I thought it was there,
Now it's gone.

I assumed it was
Attached to me,
That it actually
Hung true.
I'd hoped it was stuck
Very firmly on.
Maybe we needed
Some glue.

It used to trail
Right behind me,
Always tailing along.
My little extra

Christopher Robin
Goes to School

"Promise me something, Pooh." Christopher Robin was being very serious. "Promise to remember that you're braver than you believe, and stronger than you seem, and smarter than you think."

Pooh laughed. "That's easy," he said. "I'm braver than the bees, and stranger than a dream, and smarter than . . . than what? Oh bother."

According to Christopher Robin, it goes like this:
You're braver than you believe, and stronger
than you seem, and smarter than you think.

"Oh, Pooh." Christopher Robin sighed. "Just try to remember that I'll always be with you."

"I can remember that," Pooh said.

"I'll always be with you." Christopher Robin gave Pooh a hug. "Even when I'm not."

Friends can be there for you, whether
or not they're there with you.

Then autumn came. Leaves began to fall, and fall, and fall. The air was crisp and a brisk wind swept the leaves along through the Hundred-Acre Wood.

Pooh found a pot of honey on his doorstep. The pot came with a bow around it, and a note. It looked like a present, especially considering the bow, but Pooh didn't know if it was for him.

It's best not to eat a present until you know whose present it is.

When Pooh showed the pot of honey to his friends, Rabbit asked: "Why don't you read the note?"

"Oh," said Pooh, who couldn't. He passed the note to Owl.

"Um, humm . . . dear me!" Owl cleared his throat importantly and announced, "Christopher Robin has gone to Skull."

"Skull!" Tigger gasped. "Are you sure?"

Owl frowned. "What else can S-C-H-O-O-L spell?"

Even those with lots of brain
sometimes make mistakes.

Owl drew a complicated map to show the way to Skull (though he decided not to go there). Kanga needed to stay home with Roo (who had an itchy throat). That left Rabbit, Tigger, Pooh, Piglet, and also Eeyore to rescue Christopher Robin.

"Thanks for noticin' me," Eeyore said in his gloomiest way.

Rabbit thought he'd better get something straight right away with Tigger. "No bouncing," he warned as they started down the path. "This is an important quest."

When on an important quest,
bouncing may not be allowed.

Before they had gotten very far, Rabbit stopped.

"According to the map," Rabbit said, "we should be right here."

"And where's that?" Tigger wanted to know.

Rabbit pointed to one place on the map and another. "Here is right smack in the middle of this and that."

"We're lost," Pooh said.

"Rabbits never get lost," Rabbit snapped.

"We're lost," Eeyore groaned.

"Lost," Piglet agreed.

If you're between this and that and here
and there, you might be completely lost.

When Christopher Robin got home from school, he discovered they were all missing. He set off at once to find them.

It wasn't hard. There were paw prints everywhere. The prints led (more or less) straight to Skull Cave. And his friends were there.

If you don't mind being found, make
sure to leave lots of paw prints.

As Christopher Robin hugged everyone, there came
a terrible sound. It was a rumbling noise, a grrr-ahhh
grumble, and it was scary.

"It's v-v-very loud!" Rabbit shivered. "Close, too!"

"Whatever it is, it's coming to get us," Eeyore said glumly.
"It figures."

Tigger held Piglet close. "You can worry now, little
buddy," he told Piglet. "I think it's a Skullasaurus!"

Piglet closed his eyes and waited for the worst.

When things get very scary (and when
you're very small) it's comforting to
shut your eyes and hold on to a friend.

Christopher Robin giggled. "That's no skullawhatever! That's the sound of a rumbly tumbly in a hungry bear." He poked Pooh in the belly, and the belly growled again.

Pooh still carried the pot of honey with the bow. "Speaking of rumbly tummies . . ." Pooh held out the honeypot. "Who is this present for?"

Christopher Robin smiled at him. "Silly bear," he said. "That present was meant for you."

"Good," said Pooh. "It seems I'm feeling a little eleven o'clockish."

If you're feeling eleven o'clockish,
honey might just hit the spot.

According to the Map

("As a Rule" . . . Reprise)

According to the map,
We're in the right place
So where are we?
According to the map,
We're right where we are
But where are we?

We went hither and thither
And yon and yonder. Let's
Wait here while I ponder
The map. We took
The right turn

We went the right way
We should be right here
So where are we?

As a rule . . .
Rabbits don't get lost
Rabbits won't get lost
As a rule . . .
Rabbits never ever get lost
That's why I have the map.

We went hither and thither,
To yon and yonder. So stop
Here while I ponder the map
We took the right turn,
We went the right way

We should be right here
Right where we should be . . .
But where are we?

How Long Is Forever?

Hum dee da dum

Hum dee da dum

O hum dee da dum

Hum dee da da dum

Pooh was stuck. He wasn't sure exactly where this hum was going, if at all, or if it should, so when Christopher Robin arrived it was a relief.

✦ If a hum really should, it could later on. ✦

"Let's go, Pooh Bear," said Christopher Robin.

"Of course," Pooh answered. "Go where?"

Christopher Robin shrugged. "Nowhere."

Pooh nodded. He padded alongside Christopher Robin, happy to be going nowhere.

Nowhere is a wonderful place—especially
when you're beside your best friend.

"I like wandering," Christopher Robin told Pooh. "And I like doing nothing."

Pooh thought he liked those things, too. It made him feel like humming.

Where will we?
Where won't we?
When will we?
When won't we?
Wherever we go,
Whenever or so,
Together we'll go!

It wouldn't have made much sense to someone with
brain, like Rabbit or Owl. But Pooh's hum made a nice sort
of whuffing sound with all those "wheres" and "whens."

There's no rule that says a
hum has to make sense.

After Pooh had whuffed for a while, he asked, "When do you do nothing?"

"Nothing happens when someone says to you, 'What are you off to do?' And you tell them, 'Oh, nothing.' Then you go and do it."

"I see," Pooh said. "So, that's when."

When someone asks what you're going
to do, you can always say, "Oh, nothing."

Together they wandered, which seemed rather lazy and sweet. Christopher Robin began to talk about education and brain and all about his new school.

"They won't let me go on doing nothing forever," Christopher Robin said.

"Who won't?"

"Them." Christopher Robin laughed. "Silly old bear."

Sometimes sweetness
feels somehow sad.

"Pooh, you do know I'll love you forever?"

Pooh looked up. "How long is forever, Christopher Robin?"

"Very long," Christopher Robin told him.

Pooh thought of long things: Kanga's tail, a high Tigger bounce, tall trees that stretched to the sky, the calm river slipping by. "Longer than the river?"

"I think so," Christopher Robin said.

✳ Forever is very long. ✳

"You won't forget me, will you?" Christopher Robin asked. "Not even when I'm a hundred?"

Pooh promised, "I won't forget you."

Christopher Robin took his paw. "So, let's go," he said.

"Where?" said Pooh.

"Anywhere!" Christopher Robin set off. "Or nowhere. It really doesn't matter."

Wherever they go, whenever, whatever they do
(even if they grow up), a boy and his bear
will always share something very special.

How Long Is Forever?

How long is forever?
How long will you love me?
How long can friends
Be friends till the end?
How long is forever then?

Forever is ever so long . . .
Forever is for ever long!

For so long as there's honey,
For as long as sun is sunny,
So long as days are hummy,
Friends can be true friends
For forever and for ever.

Real love is ever so strong . . .
Friendship is forever long.